GOOD GREETINGS!

Magnificent Moon Hare here!

As you are reading this book, that makes you very magnificent too, but before you start reading it you need to know a bit about STUFF and THINGS. STUFF is very important and there's a lot of it in this book and also there are a lot of THINGS too.

1. THINGS.

In this Brilliant Book there's a Dragon and a P.J. (that's a Person and she's just A BIT BOSSY) and an Elsiness and a Kingy (two in fact) but most importantly of all there's a ME.

2. STUFF.

The best sort of STUFF is the STUFF that I can STUFF into my stripy tights. I am the Magnificent Moon Hare and I live in the moon. I do really actually and if you look up at a full moon, you will see me.

3. IMPORTANT STUFF.

You will not see me if you look DOWN. You must look UP. Now, lots of people can't see me and that's because they're not using their EYES. It's very important to use your EYES if you're looking for STUFF and not your EARS, cos that won't work. So next time the moon is full (that's roundy with no gaps or bendy bits), then look up and say GOOD GREETINGS!

4. MORE THINGS.

THINGS happen in this book, so you had better start reading it or they will have HAPPENED and you'll have missed them. If when you're reading it, STUFF tries to happen and gets in the way, like you need to go on an Adventure or Rescue Someone or something, take this Magnificent Book with you and you will Always Have It.

EGMONT

We bring stories to life

The Magnificent Moon Hare first published in Great Britain 2012
by Egmont UK Limited
239 Kensington High Street
London W8 6SA

Text copyright © Sue Monroe 2012
Illustrations copyright © Birgitta Sif 2012

ISBN 978 1 4052 5875 3

1 3 5 7 9 10 8 6 4 2

A CIP catalogue record for this title is available from the British Library

Printed and bound in Great Britain by the CPI Group

48993/1

EGMONT LUCKY COIN

Our story began over a century ago, when seventeen-year-old Egmont Harald Petersen found a coin in the street.

He was on his way to buy a flyswatter, a small hand-operated printing machine that he then set up in his tiny apartment.

The coin brought him such good luck that today Egmont has offices in over 30 countries around the world. And that lucky coin is still kept at the company's head offices in Denmark.

The Magnificent Moon Hare

by **SUE MONROE**

Illustrated by
Birgitta Sif

EGMONT

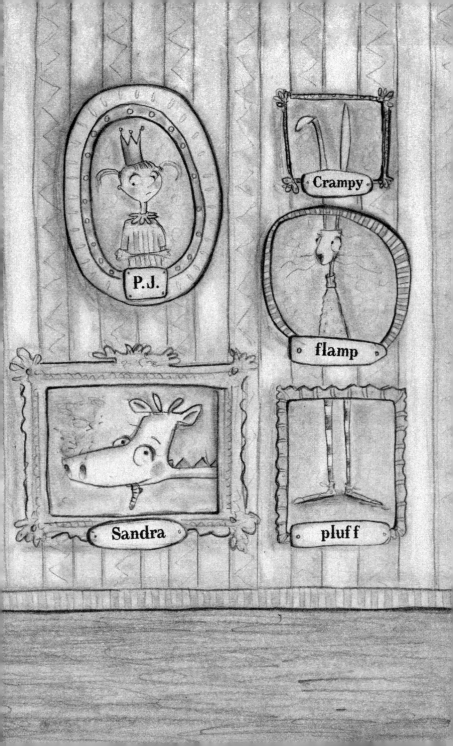

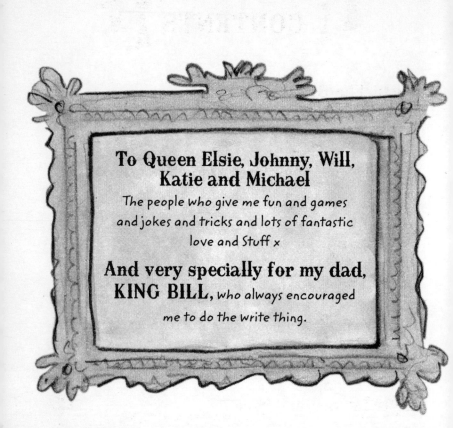

To Queen Elsie, Johnny, Will, Katie and Michael

The people who give me fun and games and jokes and tricks and lots of fantastic love and Stuff x

And very specially for my dad, KING BILL, who always encouraged me to do the write thing.

CONTENTS

One: The Beginning   1

Two: Allsorts of Trouble   21

Three: The Magnificent, Fantabulously
Famous Moon Hare   31

Four: Sandra's Story   56

Five: The Amazing Middle   67

Six: Spectacles, Squishings and Strawberry Jam   84

Seven: Chess Bored   112

Eight: Picnics and Panic   133

Nine: Chess Peace   145

Ten: Hare Today, Gone Tomorrow   160

Eleven: The End . . . ?   178

Twelve: The Beginning (Again)   187

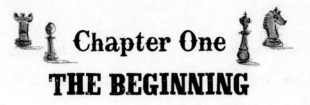

Chapter One
THE BEGINNING

P.J. Petulant scowled. It was a dangerous scowl. The sort of scowl that made her servants hide, the sort of scowl that made the Royal Nanny's knees knock together and the sort of scowl that Meant Trouble.

Her father, King Winston Petulant, the king of Outlandish, knew that scowl. He felt his throat go very dry.

'Now P.J., my love,' he began, 'you know that it just isn't possible.'

King Winston was sitting at his chess

table in the throne room. The board was laid out and he was in the middle of a game. He moved a piece, a white knight, very slightly to the left and then quickly put it back again.

P.J.'s scowl deepened.

Queen Elsie Petulant had an idea. 'How about a nice goldfish instead?'

'I don't want a goldfish,' P.J. said quietly.

'I WANT A DRAGON!'

she added loudly.

'Inside voice please, Petunia dear.' The queen sat on the throne with a hand to her throbbing temple.

'Don't call me that! You always call me that when I can't do something! My name is P.J.!' shouted P.J., not using her inside voice at all.

'Oh, don't be silly, dear,' said the

queen, ignoring the danger. 'Petunia Joy is a pretty name.'

'It's stooopid!' snapped P.J., crossing her arms.

'You were named Petunia after your great, great, great, great, great grandmother who went to explore in Africa and was never seen again. And if you remember, we called you Joy because you were always such a happy smiley baby,' said Queen Elsie. 'Then you grew up,' she added.

'People used to comment on it,' said King Winston. 'She must be the smiliest baby in all Outlandish, they'd say.'

'And she was,' agreed the queen.

P.J. could sense that her parents were losing track of the conversation and so she decided to remind them where they had got to.

'I WANT A DRAGON!'

she yelled.

'Please be reasonable, P.J. my dove,' pleaded the king, looking anxiously at the queen. She was sitting on his throne rather than her own, a thing that always slightly annoyed the king and made him feel uncomfortable.

'Dragons are very difficult to come by,' continued the queen. 'Especially after that . . . incident with your cousin Bill.'

'Yes,' said the king. 'Very unfortunate and unexpected after all the training that he'd given the beast.' He moved from the table to the side of the queen and cleared his throat a little.

Why did she always sit on his throne?

'Cousin Bill didn't know the first thing about dragons. A dragon would never eat me,' said P.J. firmly.

King Winston agreed. *It'd have to be a pretty brave dragon*, he thought.

'I want a dragon,' said P.J. ominously. 'And you know what I'll do if I *don't* get one . . .'

'Now, pumpkin,' pleaded the king.

P.J. folded her arms and held her breath. This had worked for her before, except for that one time when her parents hadn't realised that she was doing it. That hadn't been a good experience, but on the whole, they usually gave in pretty quickly.

'Oh dear, how tiresome.' Queen Elsie stood up and pulled at a long piece of fabric next to the king's throne. Somewhere far off in the castle, a summoning bell rang.

King Winston tried to slip deftly under the queen's arm to reach his throne but the queen slumped back down with a big sigh.

P.J. was feeling a little worried, and light-headed. This was taking a while. She crossed her eyes to make herself more of a concern.

'P.J., pet lamb,' began the king, stepping over the queen's feet to reach her throne. 'Please try to see it from our point of view.' He sat down heavily.

P.J. had turned a peculiar colour.

Just then, the doors to the throne room swung open and a servant, bowing very low, entered the room nervously.

'Get P.J. a dragon,' said the queen flatly.

P.J. let out a gasp of relief.

'A d . . . d . . . dragon, Ma'am?' The servant now looked terrified.

'Yes!' snapped the queen, holding her hand to her head again. Then in a kinder voice she added, 'Find a nice one, please. Not too chompy.'

'Green!' said P.J. 'And purple too. With scales and brown eyes!'

'They all have scales,' muttered the king.

'And precious jewels on its belly and . . .' P.J. thought hard. 'I shall call it Sandra.'

'Now P.J., when you get . . . err . . . Sandra, you must promise to look after her. She'll need to be walked and fed and read to. You know how dragons love stories.' The queen stood up. 'Really, Winston, I do wish that you would stop using my throne. Your own is right here.'

The king stared at his wife in disbelief.

'Now, my head is simply pounding,' continued the Queen. 'Therefore I am going shopping.'

'Thank you!' said P.J. sweetly.

The servant, bowing so low that the buttons on his jacket made a clinking noise on the floor, began to leave. Stopping at the doors he took a look at the royal family, rolled his eyes and shook his head. Luckily for him no one saw.

King Winston stood up. 'Well, if that's settled then . . . Wait a moment! What's that?'

A flash of sunlight hit the throne room window for just an instant. King Winston rushed over to where the chess table stood.

'I knew it!' he shouted, waving his fist out of the window. 'That dratted Rupert.

11

He's spying on the board again!'

Rupert (or **King Rupert of Questaria** to give him his proper title) lived in the castle opposite. He was a proud king and a fine chess player; he had won every award in every tournament in the land. He was also King Winston's opponent, and had been playing chess with him for the past four years, including the game that was currently set up in the throne room. Unfortunately for King Winston (who was not such a good chess player, but was becoming a very good cheat), King Rupert was winning. Again.

Another glint of sunlight hit the window. 'He's got that blooming telescope out again!' shouted King Winston. And sure enough, poking out from the top window of the adjacent castle, a large, brass telescope could be seen, with a huge round lens.

'Oh, Winston dear, do come away from the window,' said Queen Elsie in a tired voice. 'I don't know why you and Rupert can't just play nicely.'

'Because he just keeps **WINNING**,' whined King Winston, and he stuck his hands to either side of his head and blew a very large raspberry out of the window.

The telescope opposite disappeared quickly.

'He built that castle far too close to ours,' muttered Queen Elsie. 'I can see what he has for breakfast.'

Later that day, Sandra the dragon arrived in a large silver cage, looking every inch the dragon that P.J. had wanted – from its purple scales, which glinted in the sunlight, to its jewel-encrusted belly.

There was only one problem: Sandra was a bad-tempered dragon. A very bad-tempered dragon in a very bad mood, mostly because it had been given the name of Sandra. You see, Sandra was actually a boy dragon.

Sandra pulled on his chain and stamped his enormous feet. He breathed fire constantly, mainly to annoy, but he did do a fair amount of damage. No one was brave enough to tell him to stop or to

make him wear a muzzle and so they just
had to put up with it. Eventually he blew
himself out and was just left with hiccups.

'She's lovely!' gushed P.J., clapping her hands.

P.J. and King Winston were standing in the royal courtyard admiring the dragon.

'He's quietened down a bit now, sir,' said the charred-looking servant who had fetched him.

'**HIC!**' said Sandra crossly.

'Yes, well, he is rather splendid,' agreed the king. 'Now don't forget, P.J. my love, that he is a Very Big Responsibility.'

'Yes,' said P.J. in a bored voice. 'I'd like her to do something now.'

'He's a dragon, dear,' said the king. 'They don't do much, terribly lazy beasts.'

The dragon gave the king A Look.

Queen Elsie appeared just then, followed by a weary-looking servant carrying lots of bags. 'Winston dear,' she said. 'Are we missing one of the corgis? Oh look, Sandra's here.'

The dragon snorted and let out a burp.

'Yes, well, she's very nice,' said P.J. 'Thank you, Mum.' She kissed the queen. 'Thank you, Dad.' She kissed the king. 'I'm going to my room now.'

'But . . . but . . .' stammered the king. 'P.J. What about Sandra? He's probably very hungry after his long trip.'

'I don't think that he is,' muttered the

charred servant under his breath.

'Well a servant can feed her,' said P.J. in a casual way.

Sandra eyed the servant greedily.

'I have things to do,' continued P.J., and with a wave to the dragon she skipped off across the courtyard.

King Winston sighed and looked at Queen Elsie.

'Well I told you not to get her one,' said the queen rather untruthfully. 'I'm off for a nap, Winston dear. Sort out the dragon will you?' And with that she marched off.

Sandra looked at the king.

The king looked at Sandra, and then

he looked at the servant.

The servant gulped. Sandra licked his lips.

Chapter Two
ALLSORTS OF TROUBLE

A few days later, life at the castle was becoming more and more difficult for everyone, as it soon became apparent that Sandra the dragon was very chompy indeed. He had chomped his way through most of the servants and a lot of the townsfolk too.

'We must **DO** something!' said King Winston that evening. He and Queen Elsie were relaxing in the throne room after a busy day spent putting out the various fires that had somehow sprung up all around the castle.

He paced the throne room floor. 'It can't go on, really it can't,' he said. 'How many apology hampers have we sent out this week, Elsie?'

'Thirty-seven,' replied the queen. 'And we may be missing a footman. If he doesn't show up, that will be thirty-eight.'

'In a week!' The king slumped on to the queen's throne (she was sitting in his) and started to pick at the seams of a velvet cushion.

'Well, Sandra will just have to go,' said Queen Elsie in a matter-of-fact kind of voice. 'It's quite simple, Winston. Get one of the servants, if you can find any left, and make them take it back to where it came from. P.J. hasn't even looked at that dragon since you got it for her, meanwhile we're running out of staff and there aren't many who are willing to take the job.'

'The castle does seem rather quiet,' the king agreed. 'I had to make my own beans on toast this evening. No idea where Cook has gone. Luckily I have a secret supply of liquorice allsorts hidden in my underwear drawer.'

'Not any more, dear,' said the queen.

The king slumped even further into his throne, still picking at the velvet cushion.

Queen Elsie stood up, walked over to the open door and bellowed, '**P.J.!**', making the king jump and the windows rattle.

'Yes?' P.J. arrived, smiling sweetly.

'Your father wants to talk to you,' said the queen.

'Yes, Dad?' P.J. skipped over to her father, who was now pulling the stuffing out of the velvet cushion and looking very unhappy.

'Now, P.J. my turtle dove,' began the king. 'Your mother and I need to talk to you about . . . umm . . . Sandra.'

'Who?' asked P.J. as she began playing hopscotch on the throne room floor.

'Sandra,' continued King Winston patiently. 'Your dragon?'

'Oh, **HER**,' said P.J., still hopping.

'Yes, well, your mother feels . . .'

Queen Elsie coughed loudly.

'I mean, your mother and I feel that perhaps Sandra may have . . . umm . . . outgrown his usefulness in the castle?

He may have had his fill of castle life?'

'He's certainly had his fill of castle servants,' interrupted Queen Elsie.

'And therefore,' continued the king, 'your mother . . . I mean, your mother and I feel it really is time for Sandra to explore other opportunities?'

P.J. had by this time hopped to the door and back.

'What your father is trying to say, dear,' said Queen Elsie, 'is that we will really have to find Sandra another home.'

'OK', said P.J., and she did a hand-stand, just for something different to do. 'She was getting a bit boring actually,' she continued, still upside down. 'I don't really want a dragon any more. Anyway, I don't really think that Sandra would get on very well with the Hare. I'm surprised that you didn't think of that actually, Dad. After all, dragons are a bit **CHOMPY**.'

Queen Elsie sat forward on her throne and stared hard at P.J.

'Hare?' she said, her face twitching slightly. 'Did you say "Hare"?'

'Yes,' said P.J. 'I've decided that dragons are just a bit **RUBBISH** and so really there's only one thing that I want now.'

'A Hare?' King Winston was puzzled. 'Do you mean like a large rabbit?' He was hopeful now. Of all the things that P.J.

could want, a fluffy bunny didn't seem too bad.

'Yes,' said P.J. 'I'll show you.'

Turning herself the right way up, P.J. walked to the window and pointed at the night sky.

The moon was full and round, very beautiful and very big. It was a harvest moon and it stood out against a black velvet night sky, which was littered with twinkling stars.

'There he is,' said P.J. 'The Moon Hare. And I **WANT** him,'

she said finally.

King Winston and Queen Elsie looked
up at the night sky. Now most people,
when they look up at a full moon, see the
man in the moon, with his friendly face.
But some people, when they look up, can
see the Hare. If you look very carefully
you may see him. **The Moon Hare.**

He appears to be looking up, with his long ears stretching out behind him, and this is what P.J. saw when she looked up at the night sky.

Queen Elsie and King Winston looked at each other.

'Oh dear,' said the king.

Chapter Three

THE MAGNIFICENT, FANTABULOUSLY FAMOUS MOON HARE

A week went by and P.J. Petulant was still determined. She ignored Sandra the dragon and focused single-mindedly on her new goal. The Moon Hare.

She had tried everything. All the terrible things that had always worked for her in the past.

She had cried and screamed and

pinched and kicked, she had held her breath over and over again until she was dizzy (she was definitely giving up that ploy). In fact she had behaved very badly. None of it worked, the Moon Hare stayed where he was.

There was nothing that King Winston and Queen Elsie could do.

'If we could, we would, Petunia dear,' said the queen as she tucked P.J. into bed. 'But we can't give you the moon.'

'What about that goldfish idea, eh?' tried King Winston hopefully. 'A nice goldfish in a bowl, great fun they are.'

P.J. rolled over on to her side in the bed. Through the open window she could see the big full moon. 'I want the Moon Hare,' she said.

King Winston and Queen Elsie left the room, turning out the light and wishing P.J. sweet dreams as quickly as they could.

P.J. stayed on her side, staring at the moon. 'I want the Moon Hare,' she said with a yawn. 'I want the Moon Hare,' she said, as her eyelids drooped.

'I want the Moon Hare . . .

'I want the Moon Hare . . .'

'Well, you can't have EVERYTHING that you want,' said A Voice suddenly, from out of nowhere. 'Although I AM rather special,' it added.

P.J. sat bolt upright in her bed.

She looked around her room. There was a night light plugged into a socket next to her chair and the room looked sleepy and still in the gloom.

'Slugs,' said P.J., using her special night-time word for when things in her bedroom didn't behave the way that things in her bedroom should. It was a word that made her feel brave on the outside, even if her insides weren't. Then she felt around for the wooden sword she kept by her bedside table. That made her insides and her outsides feel brave.

She sank slowly back down into her duvet, pulled it up to her nose and tried to think happy thoughts.

'Ooh! Twinkly!' said the voice, making P.J. sit up again.

Very slowly, still keeping her eyes on the room, she pressed the switch on her bedside lamp. Nothing looked different, her clothes from that day were still on the floor where she had left them, along with a few toys, some books and a half-eaten bag of ready salted crisps that she was saving for emergencies.

'Very Special Things!'

said the voice suddenly and from the foot of her bed, up popped . . . a large brown hare.

He was wearing P.J.'s crown, slightly over one eye. 'What's this?' he asked, pointing to it.

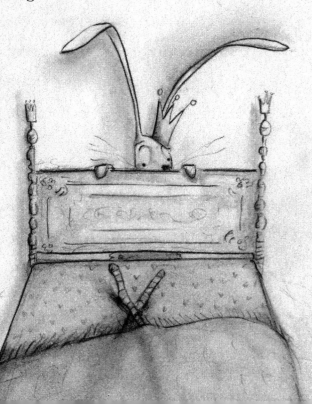

P.J. gave herself a sharp pinch, to check that she wasn't dreaming.

'**Oww!**' she said.

'I shall call it an $Oww!$ then.' He leaned over and poked the wooden sword in her hand. '$OOH! POINTY!$' he said, before hopping across the room to the wardrobe, where he began rummaging around.

P.J. watched him. He was a particularly large hare, almost up to her shoulders, with very long ears, and his soft, brown, silky fur seemed to shimmer.

'It's actually a crown,' she said. It was still balanced precariously on his head.

'I shall call it an $OWW!$' said the Hare

stubbornly.

'Are you the Moon Hare?' asked P.J., hoping that he was.

'That's a silly question,' answered the Moon Hare. 'Of course I am.'

He was now wearing a pair of green stripy tights that he had found in the wardrobe.

'How did you end up in my bedroom?'

'I'm not sure really,' replied the Moon Hare, stretching out the elastic on the stripy tights. 'I was sort of pulled here, I guess. That happens every so often. I feel a tugging on my ears and ... TWANG!' He let go of the elastic. 'You're really very lucky to have me.'

P.J. took a quick look at the moon and, sure enough, it was very smooth and round and there was no sign of the hare in it.

'I did it! You came from the moon!' She laughed, clapping her hands. 'What's the moon like?'

'Very shiny,' said the Moon Hare. 'Needs a lot of polishing,' he added, struggling to pull a yellow jumper over his head. 'Quite a lot of work really,' the Moon Hare continued in a woolly voice. 'Especially when it's a full moon and I have to do the whole thing.'

He tugged at the jumper some more, taking hold of the sleeves and pulling hard. He lost his balance and disappeared into the wardrobe with a

CRASH!

'That doesn't sound good,' said P.J., looking at the moon again.

'I prefer a crescent moon,' said the Moon Hare from inside the wardrobe. 'Then I only have to do the bit that shows.'

After much clanging and bending of coat hangers, he appeared from the wardrobe, wearing the crown, the yellow jumper, the green stripy tights and a pair of red trainers.

'Very Stylish,' said the Moon Hare.

'Silly Moon Hare,' replied P.J.

'I'm not called Moon Hare actually, clever pants,' he said casually. 'At the moment I'm Crampyflamppluff.'

P.J. let out a squeal of laughter. 'That's a **REALLY** silly name,' she said rudely.

The Moon Hare put his hands on his hips and gave her A Look. 'It's not as silly as yours . . . Pyjamas!' he said, just as rudely.

'P.J. doesn't stand for "pyjamas",' said P.J. firmly.

'Pyjamas Ploppy Pants Petulant,' said the Moon Hare just as firmly.

'That's not my name,' said P.J.

'Yes it is. Pyjamas is your first name and Ploppy Pants is your MIDDLE name,' said the Moon Hare, poking out his tongue.

P.J. poked hers out back at him.

The Moon Hare hopped over to the half-eaten bag of ready salted crisps and began to munch on them.

'You have a floordrobe,' he said with his mouth full, pointing to the clothes that had been left on the floor and spitting bits of crisp all over the carpet.

'Yuk!' he continued, scraping his tongue with a paw and pulling a face. 'I don't like crispy cardboard.' And he spat the rest of the crisps back into the bag. 'Anyway, now I'm here, which is *very* lucky for you, what are we going to do?'

'What do you mean?' asked P.J., remembering never to touch the crisp packet again.

'I W*A*N*T* fun and games and jokes and tricks and lots of F*A*N*T*A*S*T*I*C* stuff,' said the Moon Hare, hopping up and down on the spot.

'Well, it is supposed to be bedtime at the moment,' said P.J., although she didn't feel very sleepy at all now.

'Oh, bedtime isn't for an adventurer like me!' said the Moon Hare. 'I'm dressed and ready to do *stuff*! What shall we play with? Ooh! I know, what about that dragon Sandra? Why don't we go and see him?'

'Oh, she's a bit grumpy actually,' said P.J. 'Dad had her put in the stables until she has to go back because she kept on eating people. I don't know what the fuss was all about, she didn't eat *many* people.'

'It's what dragons do,' agreed the Moon Hare. 'If you don't read them bedtime stories they're very Unmanageable and Unpredictable.'

'I don't think anyone has read to her at all,' said P.J., trying not to look guilty. 'I didn't know that you had to,' she fibbed.

The Moon Hare gave her A Look.

'Well come on, let's take him a story.' He hopped over to the bookshelves, which were stacked high with beautiful books.

'Ooh! Look! Here's one with a dragon in it, he will like that,' said the Moon Hare and he took the book from the shelf and hopped to the door. 'Come along,' he said.

P.J. put on her green dressing gown over her pyjamas, slipped on her pink slippers and followed the Moon Hare, who by this time was out of the door and at the top of the stairs.

He jumped on
to the banisters and
slid all the way down, yelling, 'WHEEE!'

'Sssh!' said P.J., running down the
stairs after him. 'Everyone will hear you!'

Just then, the doors to the throne

room swung open. P.J. quickly pulled the Moon Hare into the shadows by the foot of the stairs.

They could see a tall, thin figure silhouetted in the doorway.

'You, sir, are a cheat!' It was King Rupert of Questaria

from the castle next door. He marched out of the throne room and swirled his cloak around him dramatically, getting it caught on a door handle.

King Winston came running up behind him, blew a large raspberry and slammed the throne room doors shut, trapping King Rupert's cloak half inside.

King Rupert knocked on the doors loudly. There was no answer, although they could clearly hear King Winston singing in a deliberately loud voice from within. King Rupert knocked again, even louder, beating his fists on the heavy wooden doors.

'I will make you pay, do you hear?'

48

he shouted. 'I will cut off your head and your nose and your ears! No! I will leave *only* your ears so that you can hear me laugh at you! Ha! Ha!'

Another loud raspberry could be heard from inside the throne room.

King Rupert of Questaria growled menacingly and pulled hard at the beautiful blue velvet cloth of his cloak.

A ripping noise filled the hall and as the fabric gave way, King Rupert, who was still pulling hard, flew across the hall and landed with a

CRASH!

against the suit of armour that stood on display in the corner of the hall. He sat there dazed, wearing the knight's helmet, the large orange feather at the top bent over and tickling his nose.

With much banging and clattering, he picked himself up and pulled at the helmet. But it wouldn't budge and it was difficult to see with the visor down. After crashing into a hat stand and then into the doorway a few times, he finally found the exit and with as much dignity as he could muster (which wasn't much) King Rupert turned on his heels and marched out of the castle.

The Moon Hare jumped up and down.

'This is a wonderful place!'

'My dad's been playing chess again,' said P.J.

'And he, sir, is a cheat!' said the Moon Hare, mimicking King Rupert and striding across the hall. He blew a loud raspberry at P.J.

'Sssh!' said P.J. 'We will be found and have to go back to bed if you don't keep quiet. Come on,' she continued. 'The stables are this way.'

'Oh goody!' boomed the Moon Hare. And then he whispered, 'Sorry, I'm just very excited.'

They walked on tiptoes across the hall and to the kitchen. Once in the kitchen, the Moon Hare hopped up and down. 'This is EXCITING!' he bellowed, and, picking up a wooden spoon, he hopped to where the pots and pans were hanging over the large fireplace and began to bang them with it.

'No! No! No!' hissed P.J. 'No banging! Give me the spoon!' She stuck out her hand.

'Shan't!' said the Moon Hare stubbornly. 'It's my bangy stick.' And he put the wooden spoon behind his back.

'Give it to me!' said P.J. firmly.

The Moon Hare held his breath. P.J. put her hands on her hips and looked annoyed. That didn't work. The Moon Hare crossed his eyes. 'Oh, keep it then!'

said P.J. 'But NO banging!'

The Moon Hare banged a pot, just to see, and then he let out his breath, uncrossed his eyes and tucked the wooden spoon away in his stripy tights.

With some difficulty, P.J. led him through the kitchen. The Moon Hare kept stopping to poke his paw into this and that. His eyes as big as saucers, he whispered, 'Veryexcitedveryexcitedveryexcited.'

By the time they had made it out of the kitchen, the Moon Hare seemed to have a lot of things tucked away inside his tights, including a large piece of blue cheese, a tin of baked beans and an egg whisk. They crossed the deserted courtyard (the castle was rather short of guards, thanks to Sandra) and reached the stables. Pushing open the heavy wooden doors, they stepped inside.

A large purple smoke ring sailed past their heads.

The Moon Hare jumped up and pushed his finger through it. 'POP!' he said loudly. 'Do you think Sandra's in?'

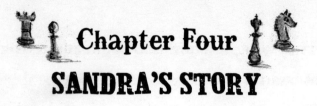

Chapter Four
SANDRA'S STORY

Sandra was lying across a water trough, idly pushing small stones into a pile on the ground with a talon. He was as big and as beautiful as P.J. remembered. Every so often, a wisp of smoke would trickle out from his large nostrils and he would blow a smoke ring.

The horses had taken themselves off to the opposite end of the stables.

They coughed now and again and looked at Sandra accusingly.

Sandra ignored them. He didn't like horses, they were too spicy for him. He much preferred the Knights that rode them.

The Moon Hare went hopping over to him. 'Hello, Sandra,' he said cheerily.

Sandra gave the Moon Hare a long look. 'Hello, Crampyflamppluff,' he said lazily, pushing another stone into place.

P.J. looked from one to the other in surprise. 'I didn't know that you knew Sandra,' she said to the Moon Hare.

'Of course,' replied the Moon Hare. 'I have known Sandra for the longest time.'

'Yes, and I've known him for even longer,' said Sandra.

'Sandra comes from a long line of dragons,' said the Moon Hare.

'Yes,' said Sandra. 'My family like to queue. It's a hobby of ours.'

P.J. looked at them. 'They are as bad

as each other,' she muttered to herself.

'Pyjamas Ploppy Pants and me thought that we would pay you a visit, perhaps read you a story?' said the Moon Hare, waving the book at Sandra.

'A book?' Sandra sat up and his head bumped against the roof beams. He had a sudden glint in his eye. 'Does it have a dragon in it?'

'Of course,' said the Moon Hare.

'And a Knight, a stupid one that the dragon gets to eat at the end, who tastes of marzipan?'

'Of course,' said the Moon Hare.

P.J., who knew the book, wasn't sure that it did.

'Splendid!' said the dragon, curling his impressive tail around him. 'I do so like marzipan.'

'Shall I read it to you then?' asked the Moon Hare, opening the book.

'Yes please,' said Sandra, and he lowered his head so that he might hear better.

Now that he was at eye level, P.J. saw how very handsome he was, with his green eyes and purple scales.

'Is *she* staying?' the dragon asked. He looked slyly at P.J. from under dark lashes.

'Yes,' said the Moon Hare, 'and it's probably for the best if you *don't* eat her.'

The dragon thought for a moment.

'She can stay if she sits quietly and doesn't make smells.'

'I don't make smells!' said P.J. crossly.

'Yes you do,' said Sandra. 'I can smell you from here. You are a POOEY little girl.'

'Pyjamas Smelly Pants will sit very quietly and listen, and you will try your hardest not to eat her,' said the Moon Hare.

'Agreed,' replied the dragon.

P.J. crossed her arms sulkily. 'Stooopid,' she muttered under her breath.

The Moon Hare began to read. The story was unlike any story that P.J. had ever heard. In fact, she was sure that the story that the Moon Hare told wasn't the story written in the book that he was holding. It was better.

The Moon Hare seemed to cast a spell. He danced around the stables, with the book in his paws, telling of brave Dragons defeating and devouring foolish marzipan-tasting Knights. And rude, bossy, smelly girls who wanted everything and never ended up getting their way, until they learned what Manners were.

It was a wonderful story and P.J. was enthralled. The Dragon in the story *was* brave and the Knights *very* foolish, and as for the bossy, smelly girls . . . well, that part made her feel a little uncomfortable. She didn't know why, so she tried not to think about it.

Sandra was in heaven. He hadn't had a bedtime story since being in the castle, he joined in on occasions with an 'Absolutely!' and a 'Bravo, brave dragon!'

He also insisted on seeing the pictures in the book as they went along. He didn't seem to mind at all that they didn't fit the story.

When the Moon Hare had finished they all cheered. 'That was wonderful, Moon Hare,' said P.J., full of admiration. 'You are very clever.'

'Yes! Splendid! Splendid!' said Sandra. 'I especially liked the dragon parts.'

'I am rather good at stories, aren't I?' said the Moon Hare. 'And I know a lot about EVERYTHING, especially dragons and rude, smelly girls.' He shot a look at P.J.

'I would like another story tomorrow at bedtime,' said Sandra, 'and I would like there to be a dragon in it . . . and a wandering minstrel . . . they taste of chocolate.'

'Of course,' said the Moon Hare, bowing. 'And Pyjamas Ploppy Pants will bring you marzipan from the castle kitchen, won't you?'

They both looked at P.J. Sandra tried his best to smile the sort of smile that would deserve marzipan but all that P.J. could see were row upon row of dangerously sharp teeth. She nodded quickly.

'That's settled then,' said the Moon Hare. 'Now, I am very tired and I will need warm milk and a piece of sponge cake before I go to bed – sponge cake with blue icing, I think.'

'Here,' said Sandra. 'Hop on.' And he blew a purple fluffy smoke ring from his large nostrils. It swirled around the stable before scooping up the Moon Hare and lifting him off the ground.

The Moon Hare gave a regal wave as the smoke ring carried him majestically through the stable doors.

P.J. looked at the dragon. 'What about me?' she asked.

'I'm asleep now,' said Sandra.

P.J. looked at the dragon. His eyes were wide open and he had begun to flick his pile of stones one by one at the surprised horses. With a sigh, P.J. trudged out of the stables after the Moon Hare.

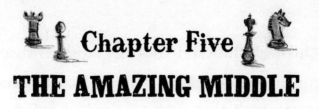

Chapter Five
THE AMAZING MIDDLE

The following day, P.J. was awoken by the Moon Hare bouncing up and down on her bed.

'Boing! Boing! Boing!'

he shouted at the top of his voice.

P.J. stuck her head under the duvet. She was feeling grumpy.

The Moon Hare had reached the bedroom first last night. It had taken P.J. a very long time to find a piece of sponge cake with blue icing on it and then she had remembered that he wanted warm milk as well, and she had to go back down to the kitchen for that.

When she had finally made it back to the bedroom, the Moon Hare was fast asleep in her bed. The entire bed! He was flat on his back with his paws spread wide. P.J. had tried to wake him, she had nudged him, tickled him, shouted at him and hit him with a book, but he didn't budge. So she had eaten the cake, drunk the milk and found a tiny corner of mattress at the bottom of the bed to curl up on.

'BOING! BOING! BOING!'

continued the Moon Hare. 'It's morning! What are we going to do today?'

He jumped off the bed, hopped over to the wardrobe and began to rummage around again.

When he emerged, he was wearing a pink fluffy jumper with a picture of a bee on the front, a purple woollen scarf and the stripy tights. P.J. noticed that he still seemed to have a lot of things that he had 'found' stuffed inside them, including the mug and plate from last night.

'I am ready for the day!' he announced. 'Ooh, I know. Let's go into the Outside Garden.' He became very excited, jumping up and down once more.

P.J. looked out of the window. 'It looks rather grey and foggy,' she said doubtfully.

'I want to go in the Outside Garden!' shouted the Moon Hare, jumping up and down. 'Gardengardengardengarden!'

'But it is cold,' said P.J. 'We could stay in and do something?' she offered.

The Moon Hare threw himself on the floor and wailed.

'Oh, all right!' snapped P.J. 'But you have to be good!'

The Moon Hare stood up quickly and tried to look appealing. 'I'll be good, I promise,' he said beaming.

P.J. wasn't sure she believed him but

she got dressed hurriedly. All the while, the Moon Hare danced around shouting, 'Outside Garden! Outside Garden!'

The Outside Garden was very large and beautifully kept. It was still rather foggy but that didn't seem to bother the Moon Hare, who did cartwheels along the gravel path.

Every flower and bush that they passed had a little sign with its name on – roses, rhododendron, peonies and pansies. The Moon Hare stopped every now and then and pulled up the signs when P.J. wasn't looking, putting them away inside his stripy tights.

He stood on the grass, although the sign clearly said not to.

He put that in his tights too, but it made him walk funny so he took it out and left it on a bench.

'Ooh! Look at that!' shouted the Moon Hare as they rounded a bend. 'An Amazing Maze!'

There in front of them was indeed an enormous and amazing maze. Its thick green hedges stood tall and in the misty air it was hard to see where they ended. There was a sign here too. It said Way in with an arrow pointing the way.

'Come on, Pyjamas!' said the Hare, dancing around. 'Let's go in! WAY IN!'

And he pointed the way with his ears.

P.J. went first, she knew her way round the maze with her eyes shut. She had done it so many times, she used to take her Nanny in there and lose her. She got through a lot of Nannies that way.

The Moon Hare followed, but not before tucking the Way in sign safely in his stripy tights with the others.

They walked through the maze, heading for the centre. The Moon Hare raced past P.J. and then bounced back again.

He bounced out of the hedges into
her. He bounced from the left and from
the right, up and down. P.J. was getting
fed up; this was taking a lot longer than
usual. 'BOO!' shouted the Moon Hare
for the umpteenth time.

'Stop it!' shouted P.J. back at him.

The Moon Hare bounced on ahead before disappearing round a bend. When P.J. caught up, it wasn't the Moon Hare that she found, but her mother, Queen Elsie. She was standing on the top rung of a ladder in the centre of the maze trying to look over the hedges. It was the ladder that the servants kept to find the lost Nannies. They weren't always successful.

'Hello,' said P.J. 'Are you looking for someone?'

Queen Elsie nearly lost her balance in surprise; she wasn't used to ladders. She steadied herself and turned round rather carefully to look at P.J. 'Oh, hello dear,' she said. 'I've lost your father. Rather careless really. I don't suppose you've seen him?'

'No,' replied P.J. 'We've not seen anyone so far – just you.'

'We?' asked her mother suspiciously. 'Are you with someone, dear?'

'BOO!' shouted the Moon Hare,

appearing suddenly from under the hedge.

The ladder wobbled dangerously and Queen Elsie, letting out a squeak, grabbed the nearest bush to steady herself.

The Moon Hare looked into his stripy tights in a very undignified fashion.

'Mum, this is . . .' began P.J.

'Wayin!' interrupted the Moon Hare, reading the signs in his tights. 'WAYIN PANSY.' He looked up and curtsied awkwardly.

'Oh, hello, Wayin dear,' said the queen, coming down the ladder very slowly. She had trouble seeing the Moon Hare in the mist. 'Are you a friend of P.J.'s?'

'Yesth,' said the Moon Hare, putting on a strange voice. 'I have come on a vithsit!'

'That's nice, dear,' said the queen, looking around distractedly. 'I hope you are having fun?'

'Sthooper, Yesth!'

'Good …' Queen Elsie sat down heavily on a large stone seat. 'I was sure I would find your father in here . . . Whenever we lost a Nanny, sure enough, here she would be. Well . . . mostly . . .'

'Are you sure that Dad isn't in the castle?' asked P.J. She didn't want to think too much about the lost Nannies.

'Well, he wasn't there at breakfast,'

said the queen. 'At least, I don't think that he was.'

'Your Majesty!'

There was a sudden rustle in one of the hedges next to P.J. and a servant appeared, looking exhausted. He was very red in the face and had obviously been running very fast trying to find the centre of the maze, as he was wheezing painfully. He bowed low to the queen and presented her with a rather crumpled piece of white paper, before collapsing in a heap into one of the flower beds.

Queen Elsie opened the piece of paper. It was a note, the handwriting was very neat and it was written in blue pen. It read:

I have King Winston. I don't really want him, and will give him back to you as soon as you deliver my queen back to me.

If you insist on keeping my queen, I will have no choice but to have my executioner (Darren) cut off his head!

Signed, The King.

Me (Rupert of Questaria)

P.S. Could you tell me how King Winston takes his hot chocolate please? With or without sugar?

Queen Elsie gasped, putting her hand to her mouth. 'What can it mean?' she asked P.J. 'We don't have Queen Hortense anywhere, do we?' She stood up and began to look around, as if she might suddenly come across the queen of Questaria growing in one of the flowerbeds.

'I think that we would have spotted her sooner,' said P.J. 'She's quite large.'

'Well, clearly King Rupert has your father, so there's no use looking for him any longer,' said Queen Elsie. 'Come along P.J., back to the castle. Maybe Queen Hortense is there. Really, this is most tiresome of Winston.'

'I take MY hot chocolate without sugar,' whispered the Moon Hare to P.J. as they set off. 'I also take it with fish fingers. And sometimes with baked beans, but never sugar. That would taste YUCKY.'

Chapter Six

SPECTACLES, SQUISHINGS AND STRAWBERRY JAM

A thorough search of the castle by the few remaining servants confirmed that Queen Hortense of Questaria was definitely nowhere on the premises. Although, happily they did find Queen Elsie's glasses, which she had lost two weeks earlier, and one of the missing Nannies, who had locked herself in a cupboard.

The Moon Hare joined the search.

He found a small brass key in the suit of armour that stood in the hallway. He put it in his stripy tights for safekeeping, along with Queen Elsie's emerald necklace – that way if she needed it, he would know exactly where it was.

'Oh dear,' Queen Elsie sighed and sat down on King Winston's throne. 'I never really cared for Hortense – dreadfully bossy woman. You don't suppose Sandra has eaten her, do you?'

'I don't think that Sandra really likes the taste of royal people very much,' said P.J. 'If he did, he would have eaten me by now.'

'I think that he only likes thweet things,' said the Moon Hare smugly.

He bounced over to the window where he spotted the chessboard. 'Ooh! Whooths playing cheth?'

'Dad and King Rupert,' said P.J. 'They have been playing for **AGES**.'

'Oh, yeth and he, sthir, is a cheat!' said the Moon Hare, blowing a raspberry. He looked at the board. 'Ooh! thomebody is loosthing and loosthing very badly!' he said.

'That will be Dad,' said P.J. 'He's terrible at chess.'

'Well, whoever hesth playing with ithn't playing with a full sthet.'

'I'm sorry, dear?' Queen Elsie was having trouble understanding the Moon Hare's silly voice.

'He said that whoever he's playing with isn't playing with a full set,' said P.J. loudly.

'There's a pieth mithing,' continued

the Moon Hare, pointing at the board.

'A piece missing?' P.J. interpreted, giving the Moon Hare A Look. 'Let me see.'

P.J. stared closely at the board. She didn't know too much about chess but even she could see that King Winston was losing very badly. She could also see that the Moon Hare was right, there was definitely a chess piece missing. An important piece.

The queen.

'That's it!' she shouted, pointing at the board. 'The queen! The queen is missing! That's what King Rupert meant in his note. He wasn't talking about

Queen Hortense. Dad must have taken his queen chess piece without winning it!'

'Typical of Winston,' said Queen Elsie.

'Oh, abstholutely,' said the Moon Hare casually, waving out of the window. 'King Winsthon hath taken the Queen to upsthet King Rupert, now King Winsthon will have hith head chopthed off!' He waved again.

'What?' Queen Elsie felt her headache coming on again.

'Dad's going to get his head chopped off!' P.J. shouted to her mother. 'What are you waving at?' she asked, as the Moon Hare continued to wave.

'King Rupert,' said the Moon Hare.

'Hesth looking through hith looky lensth.'

P.J. looked out of the window and sure enough, King Rupert's telescope, or looky lens, was straining in their direction.

P.J. stuck out her tongue at the telescope and pulled the Moon Hare away.

'Where does Dad keep his Very Private Secret Stuff?' she asked her mother.

'In his underwear drawer,' replied the queen. 'But I don't remember seeing a chess piece there when I last looked.'

'Then we musth resthcue the king and athk him!' said the Moon Hare dramatically. 'We will need Sthandra!' He bowed low to Queen Elsie and bounced out of the throne room.

'Unusual little girl,' said Queen Elsie, staring after him. 'Unfortunate ears.'

P.J. curtseyed quickly to her mother and raced after the Moon Hare.

When she reached her bedroom, the wardrobe doors were open and the Moon Hare was trying on a red jacket with gold braid on the collar. It was more of a coat on him. He was also now wearing a yellow silk scarf and a hat with a large floppy blue feather that he had attached to it with a safety pin. He still wore the stripy tights.

'How do I look?' he asked, twirling.

P.J. giggled.

'I LOOK LIKE A HERO,' said the Moon Hare, 'on a rescue mission.' And he picked up P.J.'s wooden sword. 'Ha! Ha!' he said, as he thrust it into the wardrobe door . . . where it got stuck.

'I'm not sure that you should have a sword,' said P.J. sensibly. 'You are quite bouncy.'

'Want it!' said the Moon Hare, trying to pull the sword free of the door.

'Well don't wave it about,' said P.J., slumping on to the bed. 'I'm worried, Moon Hare. What if Dad makes King Rupert *really* cross and he does get his executioner to cut off his head?'

'Oh, rescuing Kingy will be EASY,' said the Moon Hare, using his foot to brace against the wardrobe door while he pulled at the sword. 'It's really a Very Clever Plan. We will fly to King Rupert's castle on Sandra, rescue the Kingy and fly back here. Then the Kingy will say sorry and give the queen back to King Rupert.'

That did sound easy.

Except for the flying part.

And the rescue part.

And the 'sorry' part.

With one last enormous pull, the Moon Hare released the sword from the wardrobe door, leaving quite a large hole.

'We had better be quick,' said P.J., jumping up from the bed. 'If we are to get to Dad in time!'

'Come along then,' said the Moon Hare. 'Let's go and find Sandra.'

'Don't know if I want to,' said Sandra the dragon when he was told of the Moon Hare's Very Clever Plan.

The Moon Hare looked at him with some surprise. 'But you *love* Very Clever Plans,' he said, 'and this one really is Very Clever.'

'Will I be the hero?' asked Sandra.

'Of course,' said the Moon Hare, but P.J. noticed that he had his fingers crossed behind his back.

'I'm still not sure,' said Sandra. He rolled on his bed of straw and looked hard at P.J. 'If only things were different, then I'd be only too happy to help, but . . .'

'What do you mean?' asked P.J. She

had a feeling that the dragon was up to something.

'We will have to negotiate,' Sandra said, and his eyes twinkled wickedly. 'Here I am in this damp stable with these dreadfully common horses, and so far I've only had ONE bedtime story, no marzipan and no company.' He sighed dramatically and inspected his talons.

P.J. thought hard. She didn't like the way things were going. Lately, everyone was bossing *her* about when shouldn't it be the other way around?

But they did need Sandra, it would seem. And he did have very sharp teeth and very long talons and she had an uncomfortable feeling that he would have no trouble whatsoever in eating her, if he was in the mood.

'Well, how about if, *when* Dad is rescued, of course, we move you to one of the towers?' she said at last. 'You'll get a lovely view and I will visit you, with marzipan, and you will have a bedtime story **EVERY** night?'

'And a feather pillow?' asked Sandra.

'And a feather pillow,' agreed P.J.

'Of course,' continued Sandra craftily, 'if I had a pair of spectacles, I could read to myself, just during the day . . . but I don't want to be a bother.' He sighed again and peered at P.J. with half-closed eyes, which made them look frail and watery.

P.J. looked at Sandra. *He's awfully good*, she thought. But she didn't say it. Instead she said, 'Dad will have you some very special glasses made, perfect for reading . . . When he is rescued.'

'All right,' said Sandra, satisfied. 'I will take you to rescue the king, and you may ride on my back, but don't let go. If you fall, I shan't rescue you. That would take a whole new set of negotiations and by then I'm afraid, you would be quite splattered into strawberry jam.' He blew a strawberry noise and stamped his heavy foot down as if squishing it.

P.J. did not doubt for one moment Sandra would let her fall and be splattered into strawberry jam. 'Never trust a dragon,' she said to herself. Very quietly.

They left the stables and, once in the courtyard, Sandra stretched his impressive wings.

'Ah, lovely!' he said, enjoying the freedom. He flapped them in a showy way, walked around the courtyard to limber up and then did a couple of star jumps that shook the castle grounds. 'Climb aboard then,' he said, lowering himself down so that the Moon Hare and P.J. could climb on to his back.

P.J. went first and the Moon Hare jumped on behind her.

'Please keep arms, legs, and ears inside the wings,' said the dragon as he began to run through the courtyard towards the castle gates.

BOOM! BOOM! BOOM!

He ran slowly at first with heavy lumbering strides. P.J. was very uncomfortable, bouncing up and down with every step. She looked behind her at the Moon Hare, who didn't seem to notice the jolts. He was concentrating very hard on removing a boiled sweet from its wrapper.

'Where did you get that?' she asked

him suspiciously.

'Found it,' said the Moon Hare, and he quickly shoved it into his mouth.

'Is there one for me?'

The Moon Hare shook his head and muttered in a sticky voice something about his ears popping when he flew.

'Stooopid,' muttered P.J., turning away.

Suddenly Sandra picked up speed, racing through the gates and across the drawbridge. P.J. held on tight and looked again at the Moon Hare, expecting him to be doing the same. But the Moon Hare was now putting what looked like a large ball of cotton wool into each of his long ears. He then pulled out a small

101

velvet pillow from his stripy tights, which P.J. recognised as belonging on King Winston's throne, puffed it up and lay down upon it, pulling a little purple sleep mask over his eyes. He seemed very calm.

'Stooopid!' she said again and paid him no more attention.

Sandra charged down the grassy slope and with a loud **WHOOSH!** he pushed off from the ground and they were airborne!

P.J. looked down to see the castle disappear from sight very quickly. She held her breath as Sandra began to head towards the clouds. He flew up, up and burst through them like a rocket. The dragon was clearly enjoying himself.

She had never been so high up before. The air felt thinner and very cold, and they were flying so very fast that all that she could see were wisps of grey clouds moving past them at an alarming rate.

P.J. held on tightly and didn't move. She had not forgotten the dragon's threat of a squishing. When she risked a quick look over her shoulder at the Moon Hare, he was still on the cushion, fast asleep and snoring loudly.

'How can he sleep? Silly Moon Hare!' said P.J. to herself, as there was no one else to hear. She was feeling a little sick. Sandra did seem to be doing an awful lot

of elaborate swoops and dives.

Just when she thought that she may need to be excused, the topmost tower of King Rupert's castle came into view, sticking out above the fog.

King Rupert's castle (as Queen Elsie had pointed out) was very close to P.J.'s but Sandra, who had a terrible sense of direction, had taken the scenic route and

it had taken them a very long time to get there.

Below them P.J. could see the castle courtyard. There seemed to be a lot going on – bunting was hanging from every flagpole and there were little brightly coloured market stalls selling sweets, cakes, balloons and plastic yellow waterproof ponchos.

Servants were rushing to and fro, and a big crowd had gathered. A stage had been set up in the courtyard and P.J. could see a large, highly polished wooden block standing in the middle of it.

A short, scrawny man dressed all in black was standing on a set of steps near to the block. He was wearing a black hood, which was rather too large for him and he kept fiddling with it, pulling it this way and that, presumably to make looking out of the eyeholes a little easier.

P.J. guessed who it was straight away. Darren. The executioner!

'Hurry! We have to save Dad!' she said, digging her heels into Sandra's back in an encouraging way.

'Do you mind?' snapped Sandra and he veered sharply to the left, almost knocking her off his back, before heading towards the castle tower and the window where King Rupert's telescope generally stood.

As they flew closer, P.J. could see that the telescope was not in its usual place. The window looked dark and empty and Sandra headed straight for it. He hovered level with the window sill. 'Off now,' he said in a matter-of-fact kind of way.

P.J. stood up on wobbly legs. She walked over to the Moon Hare who was still snoring and gave him a shake. 'We're here,' she said, twanging the elastic on his sleep mask.

The Moon Hare stretched in a lazy way and lifted the mask from his eyes. 'What?'

'I said, we are here!' shouted P.J. crossly. 'Take the cotton wool out of your ears!'

'I can't hear you, I've got cotton wool in my ears!' shouted the Moon Hare.

'Take it out!' shouted P.J.

'What?' the Moon Hare shouted back. 'Hang on . . . I'll take it out!' And he removed the cotton wool from his ears. 'What?' he said.

P.J. turned her back on him and climbed carefully off the dragon's back and on to the window sill.

The Moon Hare followed her, tucking his pillow back into his stripy tights. Then he turned to Sandra and bowed low.

'That was Spectacular!' he announced.

The dragon seemed pleased. He blew a little smoke ring and blushed slightly.

'We could have gone a much quicker way,' said P.J. sulkily.

'Next time *you* can fly and I'll just sit on *your* back,' said Sandra crossly. 'Call me when you need me, I'll be around somewhere.' And he moved off lazily into the clouds.

P.J. and the Moon Hare climbed down from the window sill and into the tower. They saw the telescope immediately. It was propped up against a wall and looked large and impressive. King Rupert was very proud of it and kept it well polished. It had a cover over the lens, which P.J. hoped meant that he hadn't been watching their flight. The rest of the room was empty, and as the Moon Hare opened the door that led out, they saw a small brass sign which read:

Telescope Room

And another which read:

STRICTLY PRIVATE

The Moon Hare took that one from the

door and put it inside his tights.

Once out of the room they found themselves on a winding staircase.

'Let's go Up!' said the Moon Hare and he began to hop up the stairs, taking them two at a time. 'Up is always the best place to hide something, unless you are hiding it from giants. Then Down is best. They don't like to bend.'

P.J. rolled her eyes and followed the Moon Hare 'Up'.

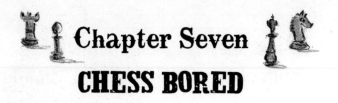

Chapter Seven
CHESS BORED

There were no more doors on their journey up the staircase, but there were lots of paintings hanging on the grey stone walls.

The Moon Hare was fascinated by these. They were mostly paintings of King Rupert with various awards.

King Rupert
with trophies.

King Rupert
with plaques.

King Rupert
with certificates.

'Ooh!' said the Moon Hare. 'First Prize.' He hopped on to the next painting, 'First Prize again! And again!'

'Look! Here he is again! This time he's holding a dog and has a beard!'

'That's Queen Hortense,' sniggered P.J. catching up with him.

'Oh,' said the Moon Hare, hopping on.

Just as P.J. thought the stairs and the awful paintings would never end, they turned the last corner. There in front of them was a heavy wooden door. This door had a large brass sign on it which read:

THE TROPHY ROOM
Please Enter
Feel free to browse

P.J. turned the heavy metal door handle. It was locked. 'That's strange,' she said. 'It shouldn't be locked. I would have thought that King Rupert would want *everyone* to see his trophies.' She turned the handle again and pushed against it. The door didn't budge. 'He must be hiding something in there,' said P.J. She paused. 'Dad . . . Dad must be in there!'

'I told you that Up is a good hiding place,' said the Moon Hare.

'How will we get in?' asked P.J., and she gave the door a kick.

'I know!' said the Moon Hare triumphantly, and he turned his back on her and began to rummage around in his stripy tights.

'What are you doing?'

The Moon Hare, still with his back to her, held up the sign from his tights that read 'Strictly Private'. He continued to rummage, his tights making strange clanking and banging sounds every now and then as something was disturbed. Suddenly the Moon Hare spun around to face her, holding a small brass key in his paw.

'Ta Da!' he cried triumphantly.

'Where did you get that?' asked P.J., taking the key and turning it over in her hand.

'I found it,' said the Moon Hare. 'It was in the metal clothes in your castle. I find a lot of things, you know. I'm useful.'

'The suit of armour! King Rupert must have dropped it there when he fell into it after rowing with Dad!'

P.J. put the key into the lock. It fitted perfectly. She turned it and the heavy wooden door swung open.

The trophy room was very brightly lit. P.J. and the Moon Hare blinked for a moment, taking in the row upon row of highly polished glass trophy cabinets, each with a prize inside that was equally shiny.

'Ook!' said the Moon Hare as he made some room in his stripy tights.

'He's won **EVERYTHING!**' said P.J. 'No wonder poor Dad never wins at chess.'

They walked along the trophy cabinets, the Moon Hare trying the doors of each one unsuccessfully. The room was very long and looked to be L-shaped, turning off to the left. As they moved further down it they began to hear a creaking sound. It was quite rhythmical and seemed to be coming from up ahead.

Creak! CREAK! Creak! CREAK!

They crept towards it. As they turned the corner they saw a sight so strange that it made them stop in their tracks. There, ahead of them, tied up tight and hanging upside down from the ceiling from a rope was King Winston! He was gently swinging from side to side.

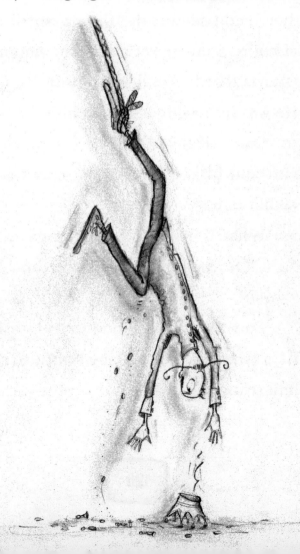

Creak! CREAK! Creak! CREAK!

He had his eyes shut and was very red in the face. As they moved nearer, they could see on the floor a small pile of coins, a bus ticket and some liquorice allsorts that had fallen from his pockets. He was humming gently to himself.

'Dad!' shouted P.J. She ran up to him and poked him in the chest as he swung past.

'What?!' King Winston opened his eyes. 'Oh, hello, P.J. my dove, how are you?'

'Dad! What happened to you?' asked P.J. as she hugged the king tightly to stop him swinging.

'Oh, you know, the usual, my dear . . .'
said the king. 'Although I think maybe
Rupert may have gone a bit over the top this
time . . . he's a bit cross with me, you see.'

'Moon Hare, stop that and help me
untie Dad!' The Moon Hare was trying
to force open a nearby trophy cabinet,
which held a particularly fine silver cup.

He hopped over to the king. 'Hello,
Daddy!' he said.

'Err . . . hello,' said the upside-down
king. 'Who's this then, P.J. my pet? A brave
Knight perhaps, come to rescue me?'

'No,' said P.J.

'Yes I am ACTUALLY!' said the
Moon Hare, and he pulled the wooden

sword from his stripy tights. 'I am brave Sir Winsalot and I have come to save you from bad King Rupert who doesn't play with a full set!'

'Well, no he doesn't actually,' said King Winston smugly. 'Thanks to me. Remarkable chap you have here, P.J. Very bright.'

P.J. began to struggle with the knots tying King Winston. 'Where's King Rupert's queen, Dad?' she asked.

King Winston tried his best to look innocent. 'Queen Hortense? I don't know, my dear . . . shopping perhaps?'

P.J. stopped what she was doing, put her hands on her hips and gave the king

A Look. 'You know what I mean, Dad, and if you don't tell us where it is, we will leave you up there and you will have your head chopped off by Darren the Executioner.'

'I know, I know,' wailed the king. 'It's bad enough that Rupert's hung me here, as punishment; I've been **SO BORED** looking at these dratted trophies all day. He hung me upside down so that everything would fall out of my pockets you know? But not everything has. Ha! Ha! Not everything, no!'

'Ha! Ha!' said the Moon Hare, joining in.

'You have to give the queen back, Dad,' said P.J. firmly.

'Don't,' said the king.

'Do,' said P.J.

'Don't,' said the Moon Hare helpfully.

'Do!' said P.J. firmly, and she quickly stopped the Moon Hare by putting her hand over his mouth.

The Moon Hare blew a raspberry and she removed it hastily.

The king sighed and very reluctantly patted his jacket. 'It's tucked away, inside my secret pocket . . . the one with the zip on it, which is why it didn't fall out,' he said. 'I don't know how it got there . . .'

'I have secret pants,' said the Moon Hare, twanging the elastic of his stripy tights.

124

Just then there came a clanking of keys at the trophy room door. 'You didn't lock it properly last time, Gerald,' said a gruff voice from the other side of the door.

'Course I did,' said another. 'You're just not turning the key properly . . . there you go!'

They heard the door to the trophy room open and two sets of heavy boots made their way along the room in their direction.

'Quick, hide!' squeaked P.J. and she grabbed the Moon Hare, who was looking for King Winston's secret pocket, and dragged him behind the nearest trophy cabinet.

The guards (for that was who they were) turned the corner and grinned at King Winston.

'Hello, Winston,' said the shorter of the two.

'Hello, Bert; hello, Gerald,' said King Winston. 'How are you today?'

'That's enough of that,' said Bert, the taller guard. 'You know that we can't talk to you.'

'How's the knee feeling, Gerald?' persisted King Winston.

'Oh, a bit achy today. I blame the wet weather. Thanks for asking, Winston,' said

Gerald, the shorter guard. Then, looking slightly guilty he added, 'I'm afraid that we have come to cut you down.' And he produced a large pair of scissors from inside his uniform.

'Oh, good!' said King Winston. 'I've got rather a headache coming on.'

The guards looked at one another.

'Well, you won't need to worry about that for much longer,' said Bert stiffly. 'Seems you're off to get some fresh air.'

'Lovely!' said King Winston.

'I meant that you're having your head chopped off today. That'll cure your headache,' continued Bert casually as he

took the scissors from Gerald and cut the
rope that suspended King Winston from
the ceiling.

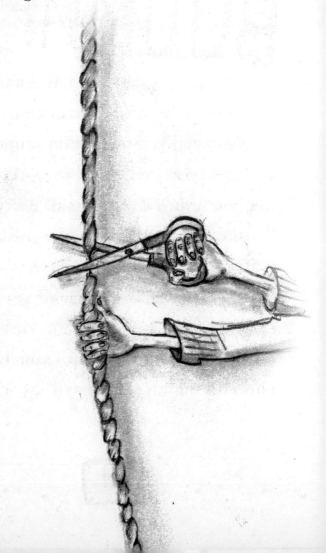

King Winston fell to the floor with a

BUUMMP!

'Let me help you up,' said Gerald kindly, and he brought the king to his feet and brushed him down.

'Sorry about this,' he said.

'Oh, not to worry,' said King Winston, patting Gerald on his back. 'You're only doing your job. And very well too I must say.'

'Thank you, Winston,' said Gerald, blushing slightly. 'And may I say, it's been a pleasure holding you hostage –'

'That's enough of that!' snapped Bert, taking King Winston firmly under the arm and steering him towards the door. 'Time for a little walk.'

'How pleasant,' said King Winston.

Behind the trophy cabinet, P.J. watched the guards march King Winston across the trophy room.

'We have to stop them,' she hissed to the Moon Hare in alarm.

'I will jump out and take them by surprise,' said the Moon Hare and he quickly pulled out the egg whisk from his stripy tights.

'I think the sword may be better,'

said P.J.

But the Moon Hare didn't listen. He jumped enthusiastically out from behind the trophy cabinet, waving the egg whisk madly.

'AH, HA!' he shouted.

But the guards and King Winston had left the room.

'They've scrambled,' he said, dropping the whisk.

'Quickly!' shouted P.J., and they raced across to the door.

'AH, HA!' shouted the Moon Hare again, leaping out into the corridor, this time waving his sword. The guards and King Winston were nowhere to be seen.

'Where have they gone?' asked P.J., feeling panicky. Was there another way out?

The Moon Hare didn't stop. He launched himself down the stairs, flailing his sword around in front of him. 'SURPRISE ATTACK!' he shouted at the top of his voice. 'SURPRISE ATTACK!'

'Moon Hare, wait!' shouted P.J., rushing after him. 'It's not a surprise if you . . . Oh dear.' She had a nasty feeling that King Winston wasn't the only one who would need rescuing.

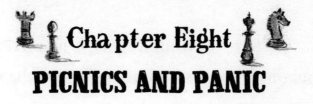

Chapter Eight
PICNICS AND PANIC

The Moon Hare didn't wait. He raced down the stairs shouting and banging his sword against the stone walls. P.J. saw him run past the open door to the telescope room and disappear into the corridor below.

'Moon Hare!' she called again and, jumping the last stair, she ran along the corridor and into a large room at the end of it. The Royal Throne Room. As P.J. entered she gasped in surprise.

There was King Rupert, looking very angry. He was standing in the middle of the room, surrounded by guards and holding the wooden sword in one hand and dangling the Moon Hare by his long ears in the other.

The Moon Hare was swinging slightly from side to side and when he caught sight of P.J., he waved a paw at her.

'Put him down right now!' shouted P.J. crossly.

'Shan't,' said King Rupert. 'I think that you'll find that this is MY castle and you are a RUDE little girl who is standing in it. UNINVITED.'

'You kidnapped my dad and hung

him upside down,' replied P.J.

'Only a little bit,' said King Rupert. 'And let us not forget that your father stole my queen.'

'But **YOU** are about to have my dad's head chopped off and that's **MUCH** worse.'

'You really are an outspoken little girl, aren't you?' said King Rupert. 'I blame your parents.'

King Rupert walked over to the window, still holding on to the Moon Hare.

'Oh, look,' he said, sneering at P.J. 'The show is about to begin.'

P.J. pushed past him and looked

out. The scene in the courtyard below was a very busy one. There were people everywhere. Some were sitting on picnic blankets enjoying lavish-looking picnics from lavish-looking picnic hampers. Some were buying balloons and pastries from the brightly coloured stalls. The waterproof poncho stall was packing up, having done very well; everyone had seen Darren the Executioner's work before.

In the middle of it all was the stage, containing the shiny wooden block.

Darren the Executioner walked on to the stage, waving to the crowd.

'**HOORAY!**' cheered the crowd, who were happy to cheer for anything at all.

Bert and Gerald the guards followed him, holding on tightly to King Winston.

The crowd went wild.

King Winston gave a wave.

'HOORAY!'

King Winston gave a bow.

'HOORAY!'

King Winston, enjoying himself, manoeuvred himself free from a surprised Bert and Gerald and began to walk around the stage, bowing to the crowd.

'HOORAY! HOORAY! HOORAY!'

Darren quickly gestured for Bert and Gerald to re-capture the king and put him into his place on the stage.

Up in the castle, P.J. turned from

the window. 'Don't you dare chop my dad's head off!' she shouted furiously.

King Rupert pretended not to listen and continued to stare out of the window. P.J. looked quickly around the room for something to hit him with, and as she did so she caught sight of the Moon Hare.

The Moon Hare, who was still dangling by his ears, waved at P.J. again and then, with a beaming smile, he produced a chess piece in his paw.

A white chess piece. The missing chess piece. King Rupert of Questaria's queen.

No one but P.J. saw him. King Rupert was too caught up in the show being played out in the courtyard below (by this time, King Winston, to the crowd's delight, was attempting a cartwheel across the stage, before being chased by Gerald and Bert), and the guards were all staring straight ahead – as guards do.

No one but P.J. saw the Moon Hare point to King Rupert's jacket pocket and then slip the chess piece into it and continue to swing gently, looking very pleased with himself.

'King Rupert!' said P.J. loudly, making the king jump a little. 'Put down my very good friend Crampyflamppluff and feel in your jacket pocket. I believe that you will find your missing queen.'

'Don't be ridiculous,' said King Rupert. 'Now please, shush! I want to watch the show. Go and do some colouring or whatever it is that whiney girls like you do.'

'Just feel in your jacket pocket, please,' demanded P.J. She was feeling a sense of urgency as out of the corner of her eye through the window, she could see King Winston being rugby tackled by Bert, Gerald and Darren.

With a tut of impatience, King Rupert dropped the Moon Hare with a bump, and felt around in his pockets. 'I know exactly what I keep in my pockets,' he said. 'A pen and paper, for signing autographs, a nail file and . . .' To his disbelief, he pulled out the chess piece.

King Rupert stared at it, turning it over in the palm of his hand.

'Now stop Darren the Executioner!' demanded P.J.

In the courtyard below, King Winston was at the wooden block. Things were slightly delayed as he was refusing to kneel without a cushion, because of his knees. Gerald the guard, who sympathised, had rushed off to find one.

'But … but …' stuttered King Rupert, still staring at the chess piece.

'STOP DARREN!' shouted P.J. desperately.

Gerald was back with the cushion

and King Winston was being helped into position. A relieved Darren the Executioner was lifting his heavy axe, and focusing hard on the king's head.

The Moon Hare, acting quickly, grabbed the wooden sword and hit King Rupert sharply across the back of his legs with it. King Rupert squeaked in surprise and paid attention again. 'What?' he spluttered. 'Winston! Oh, yes, of course . . .'

He leaned out of the window and shouted in a loud royal voice to the courtyard below: **'STOP! STOP, I SAY! STOP THE EXECUTION!'**

Everyone in the courtyard looked up. Darren the Executioner stopped, his axe in mid-air, and looked up too.

King Rupert then turned to the guards, still standing at the door to the room. 'Guards!' he commanded. 'Bring King Winston to me.'

The guards saluted and left the room quickly.

'I don't understand it . . .' said a bewildered King Rupert, and he sat down on a nearby throne, staring hard at the chess piece.

The Moon Hare hopped over to him and stroked his knee. 'Don't worry,' he said, 'you wouldn't believe the things that I find and I don't know that I've lost ANY of them.' And he patted his stripy tights.

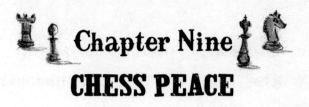

Chapter Nine
CHESS PEACE

A loud **BOOING** from the courtyard signalled the return of the guards to the throne room with King Winston, who looked in a very good mood.

'Dad!' P.J. rushed over to him and hugged him tightly.

'Hello, P.J. my love,' said King Winston. 'Did you see the crowds? Couldn't get enough of me.'

He walked over to the window and stuck out his head.

'**HOORAY!**' shouted the crowd.

'Dad,' said P.J., dragging him away from the window.

'**BOO!**' said the crowd.

'**HOORAY!**' said the Moon Hare, who wasn't really keeping up.

King Rupert looked up from his place on the throne and sneered at King Winston. 'I saw you out there,' he said. 'You even cheat when it's your turn to be executed.'

'The crowd loved me,' King Winston retorted. 'I was just giving them more of a show.'

'Dad,' said P.J., 'I think that you should say sorry to King Rupert.'

King Winston's mouth fell open.

'Ha! Ha!' said King Rupert, pointing a bony finger at King Winston.

'And King Rupert,' she continued, 'I think that you should show my dad your missing queen.'

King Rupert quickly closed his hand over the chess piece. 'I'm not sure that I want to,' he said sulkily.

King Winston looked astonished. He patted his secret pocket and looked inside, only to find it empty.

'Dad?' said P.J., turning to her father. 'What do you have to say?'

'Ha! Ha!' shouted King Winston in triumph, pointing his finger back at King Rupert. 'See! You, sir! You, sir, are the cheat!'

'YEAY!' shouted the Moon Hare, jumping up and down in delight.

'DAD!' P.J. was shocked.

The Moon Hare blew a loud and rather wet raspberry.

'Moon Hare!' P.J. stamped her foot crossly and wiped herself down.

The Moon Hare blew another.

P.J. thought it best to ignore that. With a sigh she took her father over to one side, took a deep breath and whispered to him,

'Dad, you know that you took the queen. I don't know how the Moon Hare did it, it must have been when we were in the trophy room, but anyway, he saved you. Now you have to say sorry to King Rupert and make it up to him, or how will I ever learn anything from you about being fair?'

King Winston looked at her thoughtfully for a moment, then he patted her on the head and walked over to King Rupert's throne.

'Now look, Rupert,' he began uncomfortably, 'why don't you and I just put all this behind us, eh?'

King Rupert nodded miserably.

'You did something wrong . . . and now you're sorry . . . I did something . . . too . . . and now let's forget about it. How about continuing that game, eh? I do believe I may still be in with a chance!' And he winked at King Rupert.

'Dad . . .' sighed P.J.

'Agreed,' said King Rupert. 'Although I seriously doubt your chances, Winston. After all, you have seen my trophy room.'

'I had my eyes closed,' said King Winston. 'I prefer it that way when I'm hanging upside down . . .'

'Admit it,' snapped King Rupert. 'You saw my trophies and you were jealous!'

King Winston and King Rupert

began to argue.

P.J. turned to the Moon Hare. 'We should go home,' she said. 'I wonder where Sandra is?'

'SANDRA!'

bellowed the Moon Hare. Everyone covered their ears. When the Moon Hare bellowed it was the sort of bellow that made you want to do that. P.J. was very impressed.

The Moon Hare sidled up to her. 'You called me your very good friend Crampyflamppluff,' he said coyly.

'I don't remember that,' said P.J., fibbing.

'I do,' said the Moon Hare. 'You said that I was very good and that I was your friend that was very good, and you called me Crampyflamppluff, which was the only part that you got wrong because that's not my name any more.'

'What's your name now?' sighed P.J.

'Steven,' said the Moon Hare.

'I think I prefer Crampyflamppluff,' said P.J.

'So do I,' agreed the Moon Hare. 'Either way, I think that maybe you're not such a POOEY PLOPPY PANTS any more. Maybe you've learned A Lesson. A Lesson that it's good to think of other people and put them first.'

'I never was a **POOEY PLOPPY PANTS ACTUALLY!**' shouted P.J.

'Then again, maybe you've still got a little way to go,' said the Moon Hare. But he gave P.J.'s hand a squeeze.

Suddenly there was a loud

CRASH!

and Sandra burst into the room. Unfortunately, he didn't use the door, he came thundering in through one of the walls, in a cloud of dust and rubble, making everyone cough.

'My wall!' choked King Rupert. 'My lovely wall!'

'Hello, Steven,' said Sandra to the Moon Hare. 'You bellowed?'

'I did, yes, thank you, Sandra,' said the Moon Hare. 'Time to go back now and the Kingy is coming with us, if that's all right?'

'There are two kings,' said Sandra observantly. 'If we are only taking one, is the other one a spare?' He looked greedily at King Rupert, who was sitting among the rubble holding a couple of bricks. King Rupert looked nervous.

'No, I don't think that would be The Right Thing To Do,' said the Moon Hare.

King Rupert looked relieved and tried to stick the two bricks back into the enormous hole.

'That's a shame,' said Sandra, and then he let out a large burp. 'Mind you, I am quite full,' he added.

Sandra lowered himself down so that the Moon Hare could jump on to his back.

P.J. followed. 'Would you like me to navigate?' she asked hopefully, remembering how nearly sick she was on their last flight together. 'I know the way.'

'No, thank you,' said Sandra curtly. 'I don't like navigators, they tend to fall off . . . ' And he gave P.J. A Look.

P.J. remembered the threat of squishing, so she kept quiet and held on tightly.

When it was King Winston's turn to

climb aboard, Sandra stopped him with a talon. 'Don't forget the negotiations,' he said. 'My reading glasses and feather pillow?'

'Of course,' said King Winston. He didn't have a clue what Sandra was talking about, but knew better than to argue with a dragon. Especially a dragon like Sandra.

'RUPERT!'

A loud, screeching, hysterical voice came thundering along the hallway beyond the door. **'RUPERT! THERE'S A DRAGON! A DRAGON! WHERE ARE THE GUARDS?!'** It was Queen Hortense of Questaria.

Sandra burped again.

'I don't know, my love,' King Rupert called back. 'But do not fear, my love, I think that the dragon . . . is leaving!' he looked at Sandra anxiously. 'Is that right? Of course, you're welcome to stay . . .' he added, hoping that Sandra would leave.

'How kind,' said Sandra. 'Do you have any Knights?'

'Only the ones in the courtyard,' said King Rupert.

'Oh . . .' Sandra was disappointed. 'In that case, then no, you haven't. We'll be off then.'

'See you later, Rupert!' shouted King Winston from Sandra's back. 'Don't forget

to bring the queen . . . the chess piece, I mean, not Hortense!'

One of King Rupert's eyes began to twitch and he rubbed his nose, which was running slightly.

Sandra pushed his way back out through the wall, making the hole even larger, and into the empty courtyard.

They turned and waved at King Rupert, who was still sitting among the dirt and rubble.

'RUPERT!!!'

King Rupert jumped, dislodging a few more bricks. 'I'm having a **BAD** day,' he said with a sob.

Chapter Ten

HARE TODAY, GONE TOMORROW

As Sandra flew back over King Rupert's courtyard, P.J. looked down to see a terrible mess. The bunting now hung limply or was ground into the dirt along with heaps of vegetables, splattered into a mushy mess around the stage. Sandra had been very busy.

Overturned baskets and barrows stood next to the now-abandoned brightly coloured market stalls. The courtyard was totally deserted, except for a lone figure in black, propped up against a flag pole.

Darren the Executioner pulled off his overlarge hood and looked around. He seemed totally baffled.

As a parting gesture, Sandra let out a blast of flame, aimed at the stage, hitting the wooden block and reducing it to charcoal.

Darren began to snivel.

The journey back was as unpleasant for P.J. as the journey there had been. She didn't think that she would ever get used to flying by dragon.

King Winston and the Moon Hare seemed perfectly happy. They chatted for the entire flight and the Moon Hare managed to produce two boiled sweets from his stripy tights this time. They were a bit fluffy and old-looking but King Winston was delighted with his. Unfortunately, as the Moon Hare explained to P.J., there were only two, not three.

'Stooopid!' said P.J. under her breath.

The slurping and sucking noises were so loud from behind her that P.J. put her hands over her ears and hummed to herself for the two hours that it took to make the short flight back to her castle next door.

When Sandra landed in the castle courtyard, there, waiting for them, was a worried-looking servant standing next to a large silver cage.

'He must have a very big budgie,' said the Moon Hare.

'And he's lost it,' said Sandra.

'I don't think it's for a budgie,' said P.J. in a worried voice.

The servant hurried over to

King Winston and handed him some paperwork. 'Sorry for the delay in delivering your cage, My Lord,' he said, bowing low. 'For the removal and transit of one dragon.'

'OOH! IT'S FOR YOU!' said the Moon Hare excitedly to Sandra.

'What?' shrieked Sandra.

'He's quite a *large* dragon,' continued the servant, eyeing Sandra nervously. 'And we had to send for extra silver to reinforce the bars.'

Sandra was furious, he would never have described himself as *large* – just big boned. He stamped his feet and belched out fire from his mouth and nostrils and tried to eat the terrified servant, who hid behind King Winston. It took a long time to calm him. It took a long time to calm the servant too.

'Sandra will be staying,' said King Winston, tearing up the paperwork. 'Although it would help awfully if you didn't eat absolutely **EVERYONE**, old chap,' he said to Sandra.

'We will have to negotiate,' said Sandra.

'Sandra needs glasses for reading and a feather pillow of his own,' said P.J. to the servant, who was picking up the tattered bits of paper and trying to piece it all back together. 'You will need to measure

Sandra's head to get the right fit.'

The servant nodded. Then fainted.

'Well, I'd better go and see Elsie,' said King Winston, stepping over the servant. 'She will have been worried about me and it's getting on for teatime. That's another thing, Sandra old chap, we really need for you not to eat the Cook.'

'I'll go with you,' said Sandra, 'and we can negotiate.' As he said it his eyes sparkled.

It would seem that Sandra was a very good negotiator. When P.J. and the Moon Hare went to visit him that evening, they found him in the topmost tower, which by day had a magnificent view over the countryside and by night was warm and cosy, with a large fire in the grate and twinkling lanterns hung on red ribbons from the ceiling.

Sandra had negotiated a feather pillow in a red spotted pillow case, a matching duvet, a book of poems and the most splendid pair of reading glasses, which he wore perched on the top of his head.

As promised, P.J. and the Moon Hare had come to read him a bedtime story. P.J. had brought a large slab of marzipan for Sandra and some warm milk and sponge cake for the Moon Hare. She had also brought a bag of chocolate buttons which she had intended for herself, but Sandra was not a good host and ate the lot.

'It's ever so dark outside,' said Sandra, finishing off the last of the marzipan and licking the plate.

'Night time,' said the Moon Hare. 'That's what it does. It Nights.'

'It what?' asked P.J.

'It Nights,' said the Moon Hare casually. 'And in the day, it Days. Night time. Day time. You are silly. I thought EVERYBODY knew that.'

'I did,' lied Sandra.

'That's stooopid!' said P.J. huffily. 'Anyway, I think that what Sandra meant was that it's dark because there's no moon.'

'That's not what I meant,' said Sandra.

'Of course there's a moon,' said the Moon Hare. 'There's always the moon. You're just not looking hard enough.'

'Where is it then?' asked P.J., walking over to the window.

'There!' said the Moon Hare, and he pointed into the night sky.

'Let me see! Let me see!' shouted Sandra, pushing his way in between them to look out of the window. 'What are we looking at?'

'The moon,' said the Moon Hare. 'Pyjamas Ploppy Pants can't see it but it's obviously right there!' He pointed again.

'Where?' asked Sandra.

'There!' said the Moon Hare.

'Is it that dirty grey thing?' asked Sandra.

'No, it's silver,' said the Moon Hare.

'Oh,' said Sandra. Then he tried again. 'Is it that round thing with the cobwebs hanging from it?'

'It doesn't have cobwebs!' said the Moon Hare, climbing on to the window sill to get a better view. 'I expect that's a cloud that you can see.'

'Dragons have excellent eyesight,' said Sandra huffily.

'Put your glasses on then,' said the Moon Hare rudely.

'I don't need my glasses to see that your moon is dark and not at all moonish.'

The Moon Hare was unusually quiet for a moment. He looked up at his moon. 'I suppose that *might* be a cobweb,' he said thoughtfully.

'And a PRETTY BIG ONE TOO!' shouted Sandra.

'I expect it will look cleaner tomorrow,'

173

said P.J. 'If it doesn't, just don't look at it. That's what I do with my bedroom.'

But the Moon Hare didn't reply. He just sighed and looked glumly out at his moon.

The walk back from Sandra's room was a tricky one. It was very, very dark in the royal grounds. So dark that P.J. had to walk with her hands stretched out in front of her so that she didn't bump into anything.

The stars were out, but they seemed distant and distracted, as if they had thoughts of their own. Occasionally one would twinkle but then the others would look at it, as if twinkling were the wrong thing to do and it would become self-conscious and dim. The sky was definitely missing something.

It was missing the light of the moon.

'Time for me to go back home,' said the Moon Hare suddenly. P.J. tripped up. 'Though I shall have to think of how,' he added.

'Don't you feel the pull on your ears going back?' asked P.J., picking herself up and rubbing her sore knee.

'I don't think it works like that. You wanted me, I suppose, and, because you wanted it so very much, it just sort of happened.'

'But I don't want you to go home. So that means that you'll have to stay,' said P.J. firmly, tripping up again. 'Although I do miss the light of the moon.' And she rubbed her sore elbow.

'I shall have to ask Sandra,' said the Moon Hare. 'He can fly me back.' He looked up at the spot where the moon probably was. 'It's really very dirty. I think it gets like that because it's so very old.'

'My castle is a bit like that,' said P.J. 'Mind you, so was one of my Nannies.

She was very old and smelled funny.'

They were quiet for a while.

'Can Sandra do that then?' asked P.J. at last.

'What?'

'Can Sandra fly you to the moon?'

'Oh, Sandra can do anything. You just have to know how to ask,' said the Moon Hare.

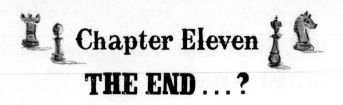

Chapter Eleven
THE END . . . ?

The Moon Hare decided to leave the very next day. Once he had made up his mind, it seemed he was determined.

That morning he had dressed in a red jumper with a large silver star on the front of it and had packed the stripy tights with everything that he thought he would need. It had taken him a long time.

Once that was done, P.J. helped him to unpack everything that she thought he wouldn't need. Like Queen Elsie's emerald necklace.

Everyone came to see him off. Queen Elsie sniffed a little into her hankie as she wrapped a long woolly scarf around the Moon Hare's neck to keep him warm.

'Now, Wayin,' she said, dabbing her eyes, 'do you have everything for your trip?'

Looking at his stuffed stripy tights, P.J. thought that he probably did. And more.

The Moon Hare considered it for a bit, adjusted his tights and then nodded.

'All right then,' said Queen Elsie, pulling herself together and using her best royal voice. 'Where's Sandra?'

When the Moon Hare had first explained his idea to the dragon, Sandra had been quite difficult. He said that he didn't think that he should make such a long journey what with the nasty bout of flu that he might be coming down with. He had followed this with a long and dramatic bout of coughing.

The Moon Hare waited politely until he had finished and then told him that the mission would be IMPOSSIBLE without him and that it would make him A Hero. The sort of Hero that has stories written about them. On hearing that, Sandra suddenly felt better and said that a long journey would be absolutely fine.

His scales had been polished and his talons gleamed. He limbered up in the courtyard, watched by admiring servants, footmen and Knights, who were all very keen to see him leave. Especially when it was announced that he may be gone for some time.

'HIP! HIP! HOORAY!' they cheered.

Sandra blushed and bowed low to the crowd.

'Ready?' the Moon Hare asked him.

'Ready!' he replied.

The Moon Hare turned to P.J. 'Ready?' he asked her.

'No,' she said. P.J. Petulant wasn't

ready at all. She had hardly slept the night before and when she had, her dreams had been full of moons and Hares.

Her stomach felt twisty and she thought that she might cry, which she didn't want to do, and so she tried to think happy thoughts. But her happy thoughts all included the Moon Hare and just made her miserable again.

'I don't want you to go,' she said.

'You can't have everything that you want, Pyjamas Ploppy Pants,' said the Moon Hare. 'You know that.'

P.J. sniffed and wiped her runny nose with the back of her hand, then she hugged the Moon Hare.

'Err! Bogeys!' he said, wiping his jumper with his scarf.

P.J. giggled. 'See you soon, Crampyflamppluff,' she whispered.

'The next full moon!' he said, jumping up and down.

'I've packed you some sandwiches, dear,' said Queen Elsie. 'Fish fingers, peanut butter and banana, your favourite.'

'And here are a few liquorice allsorts too,' said King Winston, handing the Moon Hare a crumpled paper bag. 'I'm afraid it's not quite a full bag.' He looked a little guilty.

Sandra lowered himself down to allow the Moon Hare to hop on to his back. Once he was settled he waved to

the courtyard below.

'Goodbye!' shouted P.J. 'I'll miss you!'

'Of course,' replied the Moon Hare. 'I am, after all, VERY SPECIAL!'

Sandra beat his enormous wings, once, twice and then began to run through the courtyard. The crowd gave an 'OOOHH!' of admiration as he took off.

He circled the courtyard a few times, with the Moon Hare waving from his back, and then, with a push, he rocketed up into the clouds.

'Splendid chap,' said King Winston as he waved. 'Don't you think so, Elsie dear? Sir Winsalot, P.J.'s hairy friend . . . very splendid indeed!'

'He's certainly been good for P.J.,' agreed Queen Elsie, blowing her nose on her handkerchief. 'She was almost pleasant yesterday and she's certainly less demanding in her demands.'

She blew her nose loudly again. King Winston put his arm around his wife and led her back into the castle for tea.

The servants, footmen and Knights left too and could shortly be heard celebrating from deep inside the castle walls.

P.J. Petulant stayed where she was. She waved and waved until Sandra was just a speck in the distance. Then she waited for a while, just in case. She knew that the Moon Hare wouldn't come back, not until the moon was full and spotlessly clean again. But she couldn't quite leave. She watched the Sandra speck until it disappeared completely.

She couldn't be sure, but she thought she heard a distant TWANG! of green stripy tights.

Chapter Twelve
THE BEGINNING (AGAIN)

Sandra came back after a few days, much to the disappointment of the castle staff, and soon settled into castle life. With his own room, spectacles, and his marzipan, he was not anywhere near as chompy as he had been. He was a reformed character and only ate the occasional salesperson that visited unannounced.

Queen Elsie secretly encouraged this and said that he was only playing and shouldn't be blamed for his high spirits.

In fact, she became very fond of Sandra and could often be found reading him poetry or strolling with him through the castle grounds.

King Winston continued to play chess with King Rupert. He continued to cheat, but he carried on losing too, so it really didn't get him *anywhere*.

The Moon Hare did return of course, just as he promised he would. He appeared with a THWUMP! one evening, through the tall hedges of the maze.

P.J. had been taking a walk with Sandra, but had lost him because his sense of direction was still appalling. She was just thinking of returning to the castle to call the servants for the stepladder when the Moon Hare landed in front of her.

'Hello,' he said casually. 'I wondered where you had got to.'

'Moon Hare!' P.J. said in delight.

'Where?' said the Moon Hare, looking around.

P.J. flung her arms around him, which was

189

hard to do as he was very hoppy.

'Did you miss me?' he asked.

'No,' fibbed P.J.

'Me neither,' fibbed the Moon Hare.

'Stooopid,' said P.J., giggling.

'Well, now I'm here,' said the Moon Hare, hopping up and down on the spot, 'what are we going to do? I WANT fun and games and jokes and tricks and lots of FANTASTIC stuff ...'

And he gave the elastic on his green stripy tights a

TWANG!

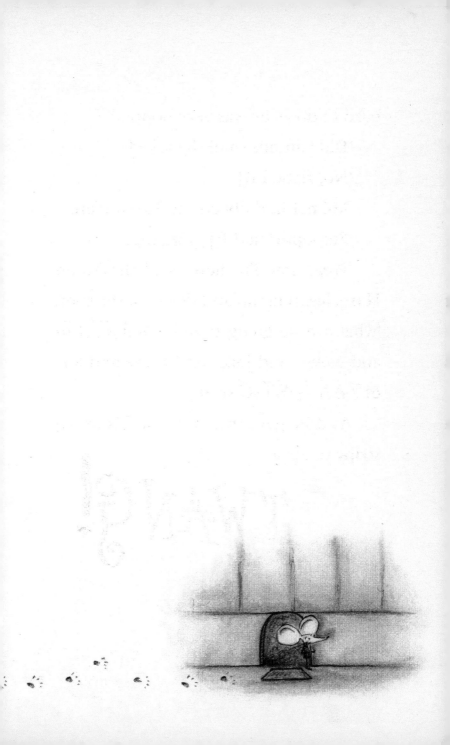

SUE MONROE has worked as a television and radio presenter on a variety of children's programmes, including 'Playdays' and GMTV Kids, but is best known for her work as a daily presenter on the BBC's CBeebies.

Sue lives in Sussex with her partner and children, and a slightly confused cat called Nemo.

EGMONT PRESS: ETHICAL PUBLISHING

Egmont Press is about turning writers into successful authors and children into passionate readers – producing books that enrich and entertain. As a responsible children's publisher, we go even further, considering the world in which our consumers are growing up.

Safety First
Naturally, all of our books meet legal safety requirements. But we go further than this; every book with play value is tested to the highest standards – if it fails, it's back to the drawing-board.

Made Fairly
We are working to ensure that the workers involved in our supply chain – the people that make our books – are treated with fairness and respect.

Responsible Forestry
We are committed to ensuring all our papers come from environmentally and socially responsible forest sources.

**For more information, please visit our website at
www.egmont.co.uk/ethical**

Egmont is passionate about helping to preserve the world's remaining ancient forests. We only use paper from legal and sustainable forest sources, so we know where every single tree comes from that goes into every paper that makes up every book.

This book is made from paper certified by the Forestry Stewardship Council (FSC®), an organisation dedicated to promoting responsible management of forest resources. For more information on the FSC, please visit **www.fsc.org**. To learn more about Egmont's sustainable paper policy, please visit **www.egmont.co.uk/ethical**.